A Father's Day THANK YOU

Janet Nolan   Illustrated by Kathi Ember

ALBERT WHITMAN & COMPANY, MORTON GROVE, ILLINOIS

To Bill—who deserves a thank-you.—J.N.

For Ben Ember, with love. Thank you for being my dad.—K.E.

Library of Congress Cataloging-in-Publication Data

Nolan, Janet.
A Father's Day thank you / by Janet Nolan ; illustrated by Kathi Ember.
p. cm.
Summary: Harvey the bear searches for the perfect Father's Day present and decides that
thanking his dad is the best gift of all.
ISBN-13: 978-0-8075-2291-2 (hardcover)
[1. Fathers and sons—Fiction. 2. Gifts—Fiction. 3. Bears—Fiction.] I. Ember, Kathi, ill. II. Title.
PZ7.N6785Fat 2007 [E]—dc22 2006023396

The design is by Carol Gildar.

For more information about Albert Whitman & Company,
visit our web site at www.albertwhitman.com.

Harvey did not know what to draw.

He dangled his crayon above a blank sheet of paper.

Just then, his sister tiptoed down the hallway.

"What are you doing?" asked Harvey.

"Tomorrow's Father's Day, and I got Dad his favorite present," said Laurie Ann.

"How do you know it's his favorite?" asked Harvey.

"Follow me," whispered Laurie Ann. They could hear Dad in the kitchen. He always cooked breakfast with the radio on. He'd crack eggs and hum a tune. He'd flip pancakes and crank up the volume. And when the bacon was crispy, his big booming voice would fill the house with song. By the time breakfast was ready, it was either *cover your ears* or *go sit down and eat.*

Laurie Ann pulled Harvey into their parents' closet.

"See, Dad's favorite present," she said. "Every year I give Dad a tie, and every year he says, 'A tie! How wonderful! I can always use another tie.' Then he gives me a hug and says, 'Thank you,' and I say, 'You're welcome.'"

After breakfast, Harvey played tag with the
dog until he tripped over a skateboard and cut his
knee. Dad scooped him up and carried him inside.

"Might need to operate," muttered Dad as he handed Harvey a popsicle.

Then, as he cleaned up the cut, Dad told such silly stories that Harvey forgot to cry.

Harvey thought Dad might like a popsicle for Father's Day but figured if he wrapped one up it would probably melt.

After lunch, Harvey wanted to ride his bicycle, but his tire was flat.

His older brother, Martin, took him down to the basement to look for the pump.

"What are you getting Dad for Father's Day?" asked Harvey.

"The present Dad loves best," answered Martin.

"Are you giving him a tie?"

"Why would I give Dad a tie? Follow me and I'll show you what Dad likes best," said Martin.

Harvey followed his brother to the storage room.

"See the nails?" said Martin. "Dad loves nails. Every year I give him a box of nails, and every year he says, 'A box of nails! How special! I can always use another box of nails.' Then he gives me a hug and says, 'Thank you,' And I say, 'You're welcome.'"

Harvey could not fix his tire alone.
Luckily, Dad woke up from his Saturday
afternoon snooze when Harvey hollered,
"DAAAAAAD!"

"Did somebody call for bicycle repair?"
answered Dad.

Harvey held the handlebars while Dad filled the
tire with air.

When Harvey pedaled away, Dad stayed and
watched to make sure the tire was safe.

That evening, Harvey thought about Father's Day again
when he stepped out of the tub and Dad wrapped him up in a
big warm towel.

Harvey went looking for his oldest sister, Nadine. She was in the family room dancing to music Harvey could not hear.

"NADINE!" yelled Harvey. Nadine pulled off her headphones.

"What are you giving Dad for Father's Day?"

"The present he looks forward to all year," Nadine replied.

"Are you giving him a box of nails?" asked Harvey.

"Why would I give him a box of nails?" said Nadine. "Open the cabinet, and I'll show you what Dad likes best."

Harvey opened the family-room cabinet.

"See?" said Nadine. "Dad looks forward to getting golf balls. Every year I give Dad a box of golf balls, and every year he says, 'Golf balls! How thoughtful! I can always use more golf balls.' Then he gives me a hug and says, 'Thank you.' And I reply, 'You're welcome.'"

Harvey trudged up the stairs to bed. All the
wonderful, special, thoughtful gifts were taken.
What was left to make Dad say thank you?

"Who's interested in a
bedtime story?" asked Dad.
   "Me, me!" cried Harvey,
diving into bed.
   When the story was over,
Dad smiled and said, "I love you."
He kissed Harvey goodnight.

BEAR-LY AWAKE
BEDTIME
STORIES

Harvey sat in the dark. He was
not thinking about Father's Day.
He was thinking about his dad.

Harvey crept out of bed, picked up a crayon,
and started to draw.

On Father's Day, Laurie Ann handed Dad
a gift-wrapped box.

"What could this be?" asked Dad, opening
his present. "A tie! How wonderful! I can
always use another tie." Then he gave
Laurie Ann a hug and said, "Thank you."

"You're welcome," she said.

Martin gave Dad a box wrapped in newspaper. Dad shook the box and whispered, "I wonder what's in here?"

He opened it. "A box of nails! How special! I can always use another box of nails." Then he gave Martin a hug and said, "Thank you."

"You're welcome," said Martin.

Nadine gave Dad a bag tied up with a bow.

"What could be in here?" asked Dad as he untied the bow.

"Golf balls! How thoughtful! I can always use more golf balls."

Then he gave Nadine a hug and said, "Thank you."

"You're welcome," she replied.

Everybody looked at Harvey.
He pulled a piece of paper from behind his back.

Harvey held out his picture and said, "Thank you for being my dad."

Dad gave Harvey a hug. And
then he said, "You're welcome."